The Duckling Gets a Cookie!?

to Cher,
one sweet cookie

I do not like
the look of
that title.

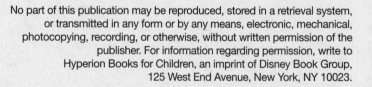

ISBN 978-0-545-81671-7

Text and illustrations copyright © 2012 by Mo Willems. All rights reserved. Published by Scholastic Inc., 557 Broadway, New York, NY 10012, by arrangement with Hyperion Books for Children, an imprint of Disney Book Group. SCHOLASTIC and associated logos are trademarks and/or registered trademarks of Scholastic Inc.

20 19 18 17 16 15 14 13 12 ·   ⁻ 17 18 19 20 21/0

Printed in the U.S.A.   08

First Scholastic printing, October 2014

The Duckling Gets a Cookie!?

words and pictures by mo willems

SCHOLASTIC INC.

May I have
a cookie, please?

That was very nice
of you!

Oh!

Look at all those nuts.

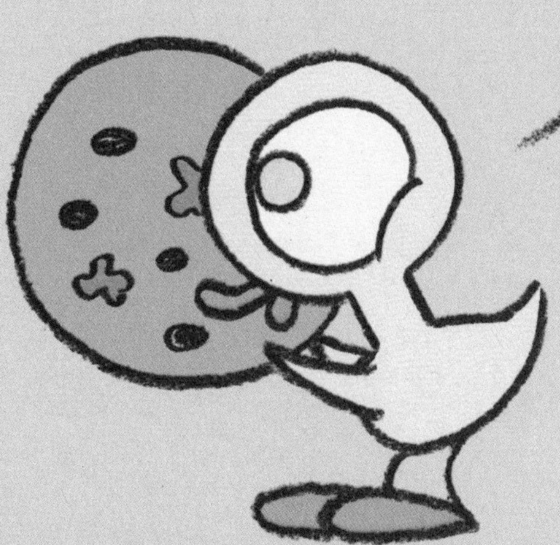

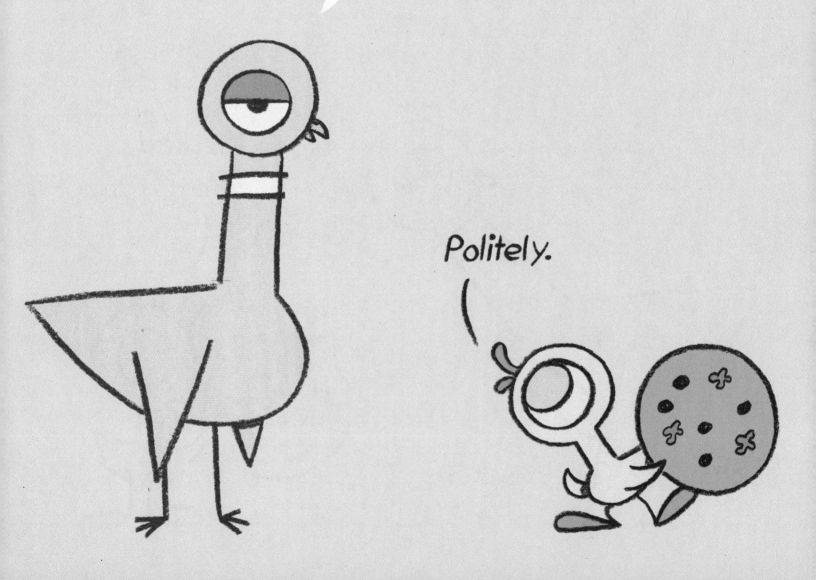

I ask to drive the bus!

I ask for hot dog parties!

Do I ask for candy?

I do.

It doesn't have to be a big bus, y'know....

I'll ask for a "French Fry Robot" every now and then.

I've asked for a walrus!

Right now, I'm asking, "Why?"

Why? WHY? WHY?

Ohhhh... there's more!

Sometimes I ask for a hug.

Or I'll ask for one more story!

I can't count the times I've asked for my own personal iceberg.

May I have
another cookie,
please?

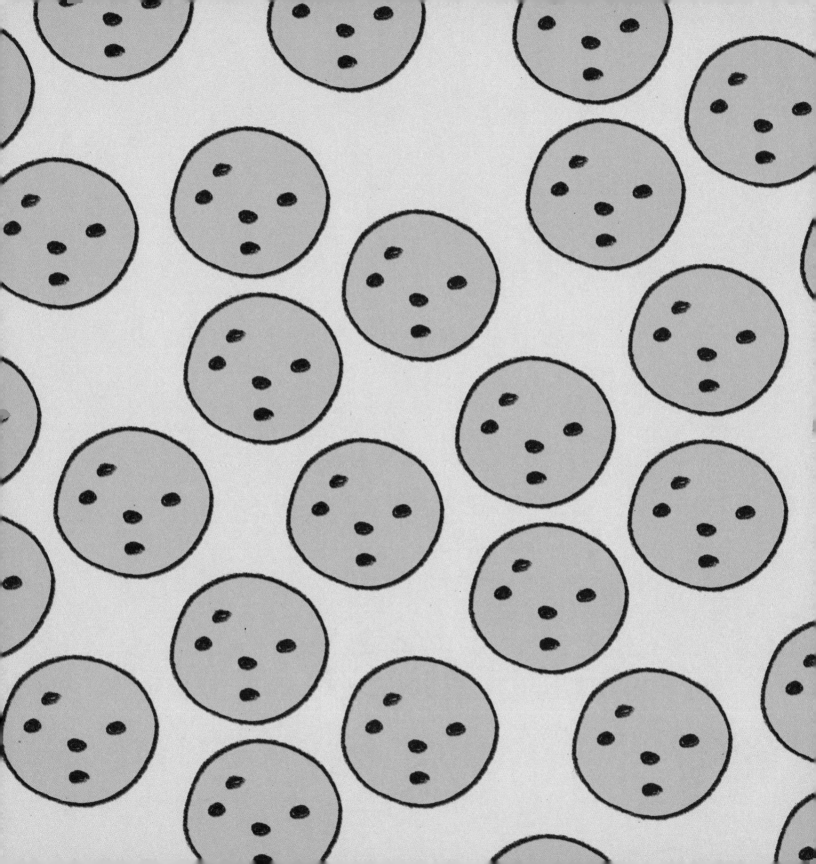

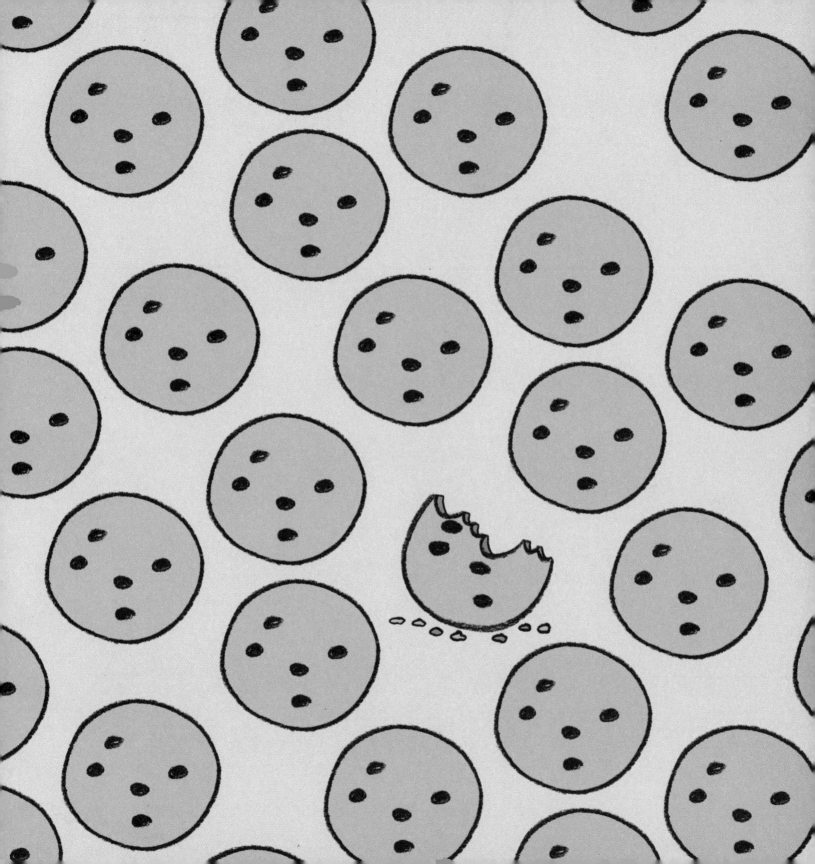